Grandpa Has a Great Big Face

By Warren Hanson

Illustrated by Mark Elliott

LAURA GERINGER BOOKS
An Imprint of HarperCollinsPublishers

Grandpa Has a Great Big Face

Text copyright © 2006 by Warren Hanson

Illustrations copyright © 2006 by Mark Elliott

Manufactured in China.

Library of Congress Cataloging-in-Publication Data

Hanson, Warren.

    Grandpa has a great big face / by Warren Hanson ; illustrated by Mark Elliott. — 1st ed.

      p. cm.

    "Laura Geringer Books."

    Summary: A little boy compares himself to his great big grandpa and gives some of the
reasons why he loves him.

    ISBN-10: 0-06-078775-9 (trade bdg.) — ISBN-10: 0-06-078776-7 (lib. bdg.)

    ISBN-13: 978-0-06-078775-2 (trade bdg.) — ISBN-13: 978-0-06-078776-9 (lib. bdg.)

    [1. Grandfathers—Fiction. 2. Size—Fiction.] I. Elliott, Mark, ill. II. Title.

PZ7.H198915Gra 2006

[E]—dc22
                                                2005014457

                                              CIP

                                              AC

Typography by Neil Swaab

1 2 3 4 5 6 7 8 9 10

❖

First Edition

With Grandest Gratitude, as always, to my Dear Patty.
—W.H.

For Mom.
To Grandpa Crawford, for picking me up over
his head so I could explore his eyebrows.
—M.E.

Grandpa has a great big face.
Lots bigger than mine.

His nose is so big,
he says that he can smell the moon.
I ask him what the moon smells like,
and he tells me that it smells just like me.

Grandpa's mouth is really wide.
Lots wider than mine.

His mouth is filled with teeth,
and his teeth are filled with silver and gold.
Looking into Grandpa's mouth is like looking
into a dark cave full of pirate treasure!

Grandpa's ears are big and long.
Lots longer than mine.

He says that with his big ears,
he can hear the butterflies flying,
the flowers growing, and
the worms crawling in the ground.
But why can't he hear himself when
he snores? Everyone else can!

Grandpa's hands are really big.
Lots bigger than mine.

I'll bet he could hold the whole town of
Paris, France, in just one hand.
But he says that would probably take two hands.

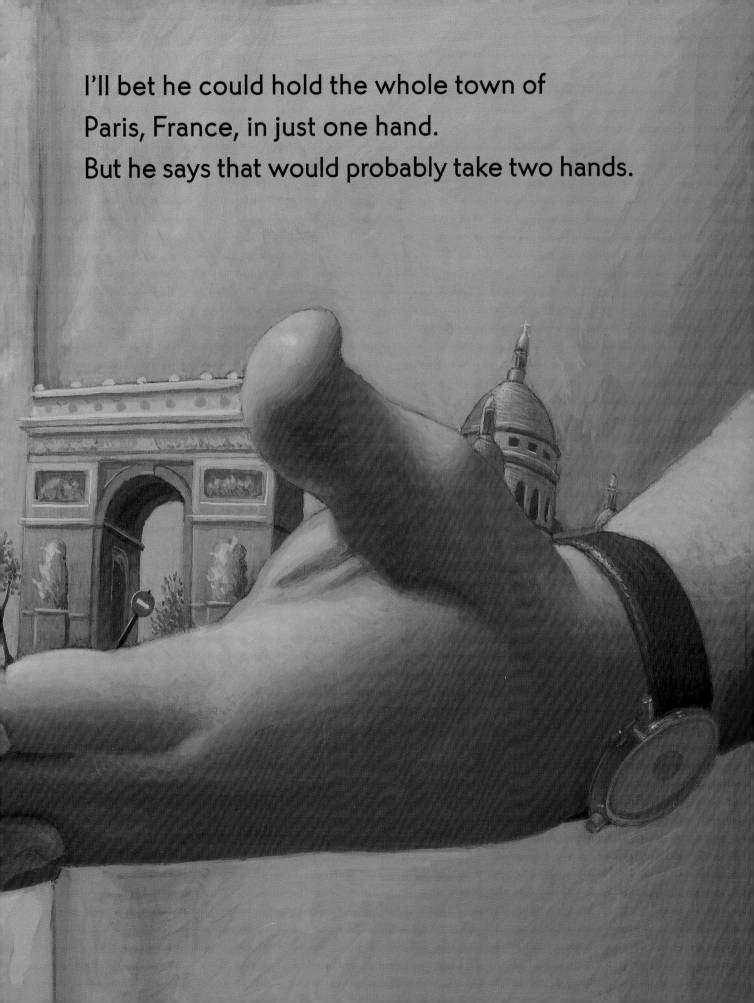

Grandpa has two great big feet.
Lots bigger than mine.

Each foot is big enough to be a bridge
over a deep, wide river.
And I could walk right across
without even getting wet!

Grandpa has a very big tummy.
Lots bigger than mine.

When he lies on the floor,
his tummy is as big as a mountain.
I'd like to climb to the top, but he says
I probably wouldn't get back down again
before bedtime.

Grandpa has a great big heart.
Lots bigger than mine.
I can't see it, but I know it's there,
because I can hear it beating like a drum.

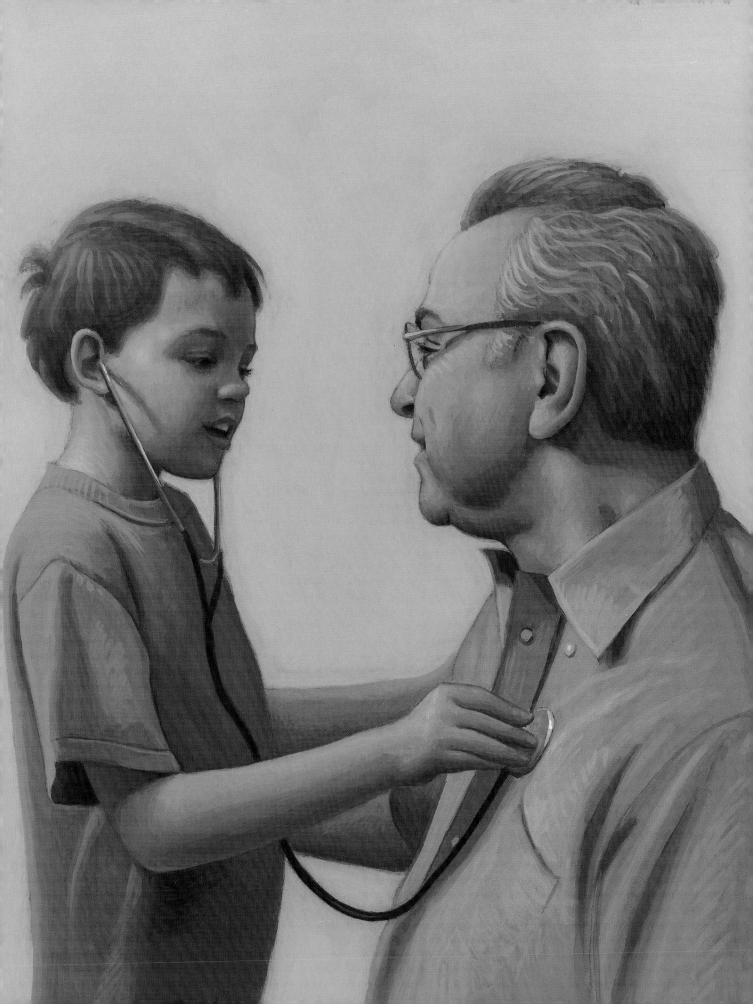

And I know it's big,
because that's what Grandpa loves me with.

And I love my great big Grandpa.